Love With Responsibilities

Evincepub Publishing

Parijat Extension, Bilaspur, Chhattisgarh 495001
Published By Evincepub Publishing 2021
Copyright © Meera Kathija 2021
All Rights Reserved.

ISBN: 978-93-5446-065-4

Love With Responsibilities

Meera Kathija

ACKNOWLEDGMENT

It is not just a book, it is my dream to expose myself as a good budding starter for my upcoming writing career. First of all, I thank my two blissful souls on earth, they are my parents and my sister. The most incredible persons I have never came across in my life, are the most important person in my life, I dedicate this book for sure to them, one is DR. S. Shashank Chetty and Konki Kamal Sharon, they are the person and the real angels who gave me a valuable chance in becoming a better writer in their anthology publications. Till my endless dignity I would never ever forget them in my life. They believed me and now I am here, to write a book on my own self, this is called a perfect guidance of beacon light, they paved the path and I followed it usefully, thanks a lot guys.

And next my friends, they are the great supporters, they never left me all alone eventhough when I felt myself down. They are my supportive power rangers.

In this book you will find the real essence of love, care, soulful and unconditional love with tips as well as stories too. My tips and stories will guide you towards a way of thinking better version about love. And trust me you will never feel bored on reading my tips and my stories. Do enjoy a healthy readings, my lovable readers.

Waiting for your valuable comments and you can drop your general thought process to me in my mail:

meeraanvar96@gmail.com

Contents Table

"LOVE WITH RESPONSIBILITIES"

The word love has an essence that changes our thoughts into a caffeine. It is not good to use love as a bait according to me, you all guys may be thinking, Why is it not good? Because, a bait is thrown knowingly by the fishermen to catch the fish, it is like a preplan effort to cheat those fishes by fixing a little gram of food to trap those fishes into the net and that becomes the final end of the fish. True Love is not considered as baits, it is considered to be the cupid's arrow which sticks directly to the heart of the person unknowing, that bow hit automatically starts to exchange the formula of beautiful emotion that mixes our conscious stage into a creative thought process, that creativity makes you a great director of your own love story, making yourself as a Prince and Princess at first teenager state. If you have maturity, you might think of yourself as King and Queen. Slowly you started to create a world admiring both emotions like happiness and sadness, Ahhhh!!!! Wait a second, Are we going to have a dreamy life or the real life? Before that I already told you it is caffeine, in our life each and every person has a great rooted dream of having a best life partner in our life. Today's generation are too fast in loving someone and like a waste trash they just ignore or skip the love according to their comfort zone, both boys and girls love together but when they find something is really fading those real essence they forget their promises that were made by them during their caffeine stage of love.

Boys start to blame girls and girls start to blame boys. We all know love is the primary stage, if it hits the cupid arrow straight to your heart don't ignore, if you are really confident about yourself and your family, step forward to the next level, if you are confident but your families are not ok about your decision in making love, have a great quality of uniqueness on convincing your parents, if you don't have the guts to convince your parents you just leave and do your work to shape your future. Love, is exchanged in both male and female, when you are responsible on loving a person at your first sight or after a couple of years, then you should be responsible to face anything, I am not insisting you to just elope with your loved once, stand still by with your partners, without leaving them all alone.

Most of these younger generation have a great and marvelous ideas to love a person, when it comes into the responsibility they actually prefer a great dirty solution which is the great trend like breakup, creating a bad mood swings, first of all balance both sides of your minds, if you are in love the foremost thing is the trust, believing and respecting their emotions. Create a strongest chain bond around yourself, maybe your friends will be telling great ideas to impress his/her with stupid filmy dialogues, useless gifts, etc. I don't want to mention all the stuff as you know everything On How to impress a person with an idiotic proposals, you champs just follow your heart, if you really want them till your end of your life, don't try those stupid filmy shows, to connect an artificial bonds. Create positive vibes, scan their inner beauty, fix your mind consciously whether they are really made for you and your family. There creates a love for responsibilities. Through this following state of my general realistic ideas you come to know how Love with Responsibilities makes your life like a strong rooted bond. Love is like a baby, it never has the sense of What is going on in your life, an unawareness thrill just makes them create a filmy role as hero and heroines, but both of them just forgot about their great role of actual reality to live soulfully in life.

LOVE DOSE TIP: 1

THINGS THAT ARE NOT REAL IN GENERAL AS WE USUALLY CAN'T EXPECT IN OUR LIFE:

When you are in love, it is like living in a high building castle. Some sort of tiny little sprinkled shiny stars just flash your thoughts, which makes your face glow more brightly. You will receive many promises, useless dialogues, and the second thing you can't even imagine, you start to change your moods, character, likes and dislikes for them. Real love doesn't expect changes, your love should change a beautiful life, feel free to express your real identity to them. Be yourself. Don't change! But you just forget this particular thing. This little mistake makes a big change, after marriage when the real mask of your partner is exaggerated you just can't take it anymore. There our life loses the general reality that usually we can't expect in our life. Love is like a question paper before attending it, be sure of your correct answers, if you lose then reality of acceptance becomes a great Satan in your life. You aren't able to find peace and security that starts to kill your inner good characters that belong to you generally.

'Expectation kills in all sorts of relationships; it is quite hard to follow that but particularly we can ignore it by making our schedule in a better way so that we start to move on; our mind never bother much on the general segment of expectation on each lovable person who encounters in our daily lifetime'.

LOVE DOSE TIP: 2

EXPECTING THE SAME AMOUNT OF LOVE THAT WE DELIVER TO THEM IS NOT NECESSARY EVERY TIME:

Generally guys, if you like or love a person more than yourself, it is not necessary for the same person to shower the same amount of love on you. He/she is not responsible for how much love you shower to them daily, some are pessimistic at times, psychologically you should understand that love is common but the emotions related to each and every person that differs, all are not the same in general. You get on to the simple fight that has no valuable ethics.

LOVE DOSE TIP: 3

DEEP LOVE NEVER FADES AT ANY CAUSE

Love is not just a fantasy, it doesn't come to everyone, it is like an angel. Those who wholeheartedly welcome those angels into their life create a world full of mesmerizing meaningful life with great satisfaction. But when you do it, like an hobby of time pass you won't get those fruitful life ever. I always admire on watching movies in which love has a wholesome of ethics, generally caring the parents decision is like a first born baby to their life, we should understand the pain, worries, situations of our parents, if we started to carry those responsibility it never crash you guys. A love should be deep like an endless sky but I don't mean it to be not deep as the sea because it has some ending point in general where you reach at the end and say I have reached my destiny and you go back for another upcoming thrill. But if it is an endless sky just imagine, your soul till your death when you die to close your eyes the last face that comes to your mind will be your partner. When you find a partner who is more like the mixture of togetherness of your mom and dad, then you are lucky to have a deep love which never ever fades so easily from your soul.

LOVE DOSE TIP: 4

NEVER EVER LOSE YOUR HOPE ON THEM

Seriously guys, love is magical but it never shows the icy blast all the time. Maybe you and your partner would have some sort of different problematic issues, it is a great responsibility of both of you to sort it out by yourself, you should trust them encourage them when they feel down about themselves, don't be selfish guys on thinking about yourself only, in our body we have two hands, if one hand not supporting the other hand think about the work, it totally ruins everything, similarly you should balance your emotions too, think twice from their side and make a solution for it never lose hope or over think about your decision making. If you have decided he/she is your permanent life partner don't lose hope on them so easily. Before losing that hope, at least think about your great struggles you have been faced to hold his/her hand to live your entire life.

LOVE DOSE TIP: 5

SOULFUL CARING WORDS ARE IMPORTANT THAN PRESENTING GIFTS

In all sorts of relationships, presenting gifts plays a major role nowadays. Buying the most costliest gifts for our lovable persons are playing a majority role of perplexion. You know what? The person who cares for your lovely companion, with whole heartedly never expects costly gifts from you, first thing is that they need a part which could feed their memories with the loveliest moments that creates an endless bound of romance, love, and lots of respect for each other's feelings.

When we present the gift, it never pays the same attentive love as we spent time for them. Time is the precious thing in this world, wasting and spending money, never bothers much in a relationship. But when we fail to spend time with a person seriously, the other half of the upcoming life becomes a great burden to live on for the rest of your life. No one cares how much you spent the money for expressing your love for them, it must be a prestigious one if we present a fabulous gift with wonders of flabbergast, for your lovable person during a party of your anniversary, if that costly gift had a mouth to speak it would ask a question to those couples as;

"I am your 100th gift in your life and for sure you would keep me in your showcase, but tell me how much costliest affordable time you have been spending with your partners these many years?" What about the couple who have attending those party, sounds like freaky stakes right, but practically you need to think about my question in a clear sense. Guys your soulful words matters much for them, the effort you make to spent time for them, the respect on their little emotions, your attentive words of deliverance and patience gives them a great strength and support for their soul, these qualities just make you feel a complete sense of purpose of living the entire life with your life partner.

When you support your life partner's feelings patiently, your life will give you the beauty of blissful thoughts that make you think better by balancing both sides of the emotions that equals your life like a balancing scale.

Now friends its stories time now through this stories you will know the value of love with responsibilities:

STORY-1

MEGHA AND KRISH

Megha was a young girl and she was nearly twenty years old. She was a brilliant girl and belongs to a middle class family. Her character readily admires each and every person within fractional seconds. The only thing that she feels inferior about herself is the color of her dark skin. Each and every person just bullies her appearance that hurts her a lot. Megha had a friend named Krish, he was very handsome and a rich man. She has been his best friend since her childhood. By doing a lot of research Krish, reached his utmost destiny and became a rich man through his scholarship. Krish doesn't have a family at all, his uncle adopted him when he lost his parents at the age of four. Krish respects his uncle and sees both his parents shelter and care from him. To his uncle, Krish was his whole world to him.

Megha! Krish called her from his balcony. She ran so quickly towards the gate to see him. What is wrong with you Krish Why are you shouting like this? Don't you think I am busy right now with my work idiot? Krish smiled and asked her to come to his home, when she was about to go she saw her mother staring at her with an angry look, her sight delivered not to go and see him. Megha stood in a freezy manner, meanwhile Krish came to her home to pick up Megha. Krish smiled widely at her mom and said that he wants Megha now for an urgent work. Her mom half heartedly allowed Megha to go with him.

The car moved smoothly and left the place with a speedy dust. Megha! Are you fine? Why are you sad? As Krish asked this question to her, she gazed into Krish's eyes and said Really! You Don't know what is going on these many days Krish?

Krish normally asked What?

Megha then started to speak to him, Krish we are friends from our childhood isn't it?

Yes obviously! What is wrong in that? He smiles at her.

It is not cool Krish, now we are grown up adults we are not the same as we were in our childhood Krish! Megha sobs for a while and stops her speech in the middle.

Krish! Sees her eyes filled with water like an ocean and she was making that oceanic storm to be calm for a while and started not to create a thunderstorm on him, to ruin his day. Krish speaks to Megha, hey sweetie you are the only one whom I believe and live my entire life with a great hope. Though my uncle takes care of myself you are a big part of my soul who cares more than anything in this world. I know your mother doesn't like whenever I talk to you personally, this shows and remains to me that we are grown up and we are not a child anymore. But my heart always finds you and asks to find a good comfortable company to rest my tireless emotion to be calm, whenever I see you I feel that I am living my life with tireless endless endings. It gives me a feel that I am not alone and that's it my dear!

Megha shouts at him to stop the car!

Hey Megha! Why do I have to stop the car in the middle? What's wrong with you?

She readily jumps out of the car. Krish was very astronished with Megha as she jumped out of the car. Megha ran towards an old lady who got stuck in her car. Krish ran behind her and both of them helped that lady to come out of the car. Both of them just lifted that old lady carefully out of the car. Krish just asked her, You and I were talking in that sense. How did you notice that particular lady far from that distance. She smiled and said I was listening to your speech simultaneously. I was gazing outside to look at the other part of the world through your window. That sense made me listen to you and the other side of the world, that's it.

Krish drove the car gazing at her with a great delight. In this situation he isn't able to see Megha as a god damn angel. He wanted to take her completely into his life but for some reason he was not able to tell his entire love for her.

Next day, a car came to the place of Krish's bunglow. A girl with high heels, well dressed just got down from the costliest car was in search of Krish glance.

Krish said, 'Hi! Nathasha, How are you dear? After so long you are here to meet me.

Nathasha: Well Krish How are you doing? I thought you will be living in America or any other foreign country……let me guess, are you still living here because of that girl.....wait a second her name uh!!!!! Hm….

Krish: Could you please stop it for a while!

Nathasha: Yes Megha right, How is she? Where is she now my dear?

Krish: She is my neighbor now. We are friends ok.

Nathasha: Ok bhai friends!!!!!

Meanwhile Megha enters in the middle.

Hey Krish look I made ladoos for you, just taste it and say about it. Then she notices Nathasha and stops for a while. Krish says, Megha , she is my classmate, Nathasha.

Oh! Nathasha! How are you? All is fine right now dear.

Yeah!

Nathasha I will be back in a moment, bye Krish.

How sweet she is! I think you are lucky to have her in your life.

(Krish O really, but I don't think that this could happen for me anymore)

Hey Krish I am talking to you, What are you thinking?

Nothing so much dear. Okay thanks for coming Nathasha, We'll see later.

Okay Krish bye. Don't forget to attend my wedding with your angel as a couple man!! Did you get me!

Yeah ok! And both departed as they finished their conversation.

The next day Krish was very upset as his company reached as one of the most top rated ever in human history. You will be thinking why he was upset right now, though it was good news, he thinks he has to leave India and fly himself to the United States. He was very sad as he had to leave Megha for that cause.

The next day he came to Megha's house to tell this good news.

Megha! Megha!

Her mom came out to see Krish standing near their front door. Her face readily changed at that moment.

Hey Krish! Come let's have a coffee.

No Ma, I came here to see Megha right now, Where is She?

Listen Krish! She is not here, she went abroad to pursue her career, Don't disturb her.

What! Are you kidding me right now Ma!!!

Certainly not yesterday she went Krish! Probably she will be on her way through.

Ma! She hasn't told me about this……?

Everything can't be expressed by the way my dear, so it is better not to contact my daughter again…by god's grace she is far away…just far away from you. Let it be, now tell me What made you come to my house Krish!

Nothing Ma! (Actually he was happy inside that the place where he wanted to go is where Megha went. That's why he did not mention the good news to her mother of course she would not accept it.)

Krish went to his home. His uncle called him. Come here my boy.

He moved to his uncle and smiled at him brightly, after that he asked him, so it was you who made my day right.

He just laughed at him and said Yes!

How Do you know?

It's simple. I know you love her sincerely, my son, so it took no more time for me to do so. I sent your following project to US and the company approved it as it was excellent. I set up a career for Megha too, so that you both will be able to spend a quality of time together. This news is already pre planned by myself and I informed this to Megha. She would be waiting for you Krish enjoy yourself god bless you.

Krish jumped on the sky with great excitement. He packed himself abroad happily.

IN US:

Megha Where are you? I am in the airport.

15 mins Krish I will be there for you.

He smiled and waited for her.

After 15 mins Megha reached the airport, she called Krish in a loud voice so that he would be able to grab her attention.

Krish just waved his hand higher, she ran so fast towards him and hugged him tightly. Krish hugged her too, tears were flowing through their eyes, these salty water was enough to sink this whole airport.

You cheater! Idiot! You never informed me about this plan.

Cool! It was a surprise, haven't you enjoyed this master plan, actually it was a thrill of beauty, some things cannot be mentioned everytime in our life. It should be felt. That feeling should connect us generally. But it's sweeter when these things just happen right Krish!

Whatever! Come on let's go my surprise bombshell.

They both started up the great career there. And the next thing was their marriage. How could they cope up with that situation? After a couple of years they went to India. As they returned into their place quite a lot of things just changed their life, surprisingly Megha's mom was waiting outside to receive Krish, this was quite an unexpected one.

Megha ran towards her mother and asked her Are you sure or ready to make him your son-in-law mom?

Yeah Megha first of all, I don't believed that true love just exist in this modern days, as you already know your father just left me all alone when I was pregnant, he married a rich girl and got settled with those families, I struggled a lot to make your life a better one, that day I decided My daughter should marry a man who will not leave her hand at any cause. That's why I hated love marriage so much, if I too select a great groom of my choice for you Megha seriously it would not be a great life for you my dear initially, but you both were adorable I insulted Krish so much with my harsh words, I made him feel like a useless trash many times but his patience and love for you just impressed me. Krish was a sincere guy, I know both of you since you were young, I thought that this love would change both of your minds forever but you both strongly believed in yourself, and my sweetie! This was the perfect day I have been waiting for you!

Live long for years my child with your Krish.

Krish just hugged Megha's mom tightly and cried a lot. And as well Megha too.

Krish come on my boy! Megha just call your mom too, because all are seeing this beautiful cozy scenario right now from outside without paying tickets. All laughed and they came inside with a great everlasting bliss.

Life has beautiful miracles that don't just happen automatically, it is created with great ambience. In love patience is important that patience gives a beautiful formula to lead a colorful rainbow desire.

All boys are the same, they feel strong but never express everything to the girls. But girls express everything and expect a lot even in small things it is nature.

It can't be defined that boys don't have feelings at all, they have feelings to balance with the real expectations of the girls. Even Though he can't express everything to you, don't make it a conclusion, that he doesn't care for you Of course! he cares, he might not express it but show it through his actions.

Boys don't think that girls are over dramatic on expressing everything, the thing is boys you don't reflect to express your thoughts so these girls are mirror for your expressive thoughts, both are balanced with correct retarted combination. Every moment of life should be cherished. In this story you could also sense that both of them never said the word I LOVE YOU instead they made that actual sensibility through their actions. Love is not a reaction of sense it is felt and just delivered like an endless priority of both the partners. A great level of understanding is more important than the fake undesirable promises. If you don't believe in your confidence level don't take a step to make a person fall for you. Because after commitment you won't be able to make yourself comfortable after that, it is like committing suicide with making you die instantly but to suffer like a hell.

STORY-2

THE LIFE OF VINEET AND MEGHA

Really this story is already published in my anthology publication and I heartily want to thank Dr. S. Shanshank Chetty, for giving me a chance for writing this short story for my first anthology book BEAUTIFUL ECSTASY: ANTHOLOGY A JOY IN GROWING TOGETHER. As an author I am very much blessed to share my first short story for my own book. And this book really suits this edition. So the story begins with Vineet and Megha again in my book LOVE WITH RESPONSIBILITIES.

It was a lovely morning. A strong breezy wind just crossed like a hell on her face, she was Megha, a young charming girl walking beside the footpath. She was a mixed portion of innocent and more sensitive girl. Her father was a lovable and caring person, but he never showed his immense love for her daughter. Her mother was not just like an ordinary mother but she was more than that like a good partner as well as a good friend. Megha was just doing her schooling and she was 14 years old, the one and only sweetest honeycomb child for her mom and dad. When the school was over, Megha was casually walking beside the street, Suddenly with a great jerk she fell down, a stir of angriness was bustling inside her like a volcano, a tall well attractive boy just thrust her without watching her. This was a great annoyment for Megha. But she cannot react to him, as that boy was very busy buying the snacks items from the shop. After a couple of minutes she came home and was telling the entire incident to her Mother. Her mom readily laughed at her, poor Megha got frustrated at her Mom's reaction and she sneaked away.

Next day as usual she went to school, that particular moment she was shocked to see the same Boy come to her school. After that smacking incident she had a little crush and quite a good impression on him. Even though she was angry at him first, she liked him. His name was Vineet and he was 15 years old, quiet one year older than Megha. This boy was a complete book of naughty encyclopedia person, a good basketball player, help others without any expectations, mostly he was so attractive and good looking handsome guy, who was more famous among all the girls and totally, he was like a dream boy for each and every girls studying in the school.

He was quiet while making decisions and he was a kind of smart working boy. A new student to that school, within a week he became an all rounder superstar among the students as well as the teachers all loved him like anything.

One day when Vineet was playing basketball on the court, suddenly someone distracted him like a blow of wind, none other than, it was Megha starring on the badminton players in the ground but no one was ready to give her the chance to play, she was waiting for nearly twenty minutes. Noticing this, Vineet came forward to Megha and asked her 'WHY ARE YOU NOT PLAYING AND GIVING ALL YOUR CHANCES TO THEM?' As Megha turned back her soul had a great beautiful freezy ecstasy that she cannot explain in her own words, she wasn't able to answer his question and was just babbling like an ideal sound horn on the traffic road. Her mind was checking so many times like OH MY GOD!!! Is it really Vineet talking to me? At the same time, Vineet just bent down to tie his shoe lays, Megha was smiling like anything, and he asked her DO YOU PLAY BASKETBALL? Megha said that, 'I LOVE THE GAME! But don't know the exact rules and regulation of the game'.

Then Vineet asked her, "If you are free I'll teach you how to play basketball if you are comfortable with it". Megha took a great sigh of relief and she said YES! Without any hesitation. Vineet smiled at her and sneaked away. When the school was over Megha ran like a breezy cold air so faster the way to her home. She was very happy with the incident of Vineet, she hugged her mom, kissed her dad and ran to her room. It was so strange to her parents. When she was going to sleep her mom asked, "Why are you so happy today? Any good news my sweetie! But Megha said, 'No Mom, Today I was happy but I don't know the exact reason', *she was like her father never shows her emotional thoughts and never shares anything to her parents.*

But her Mother was 'Her Mother' she never expected her to tell all the running thoughts to her, instead she understands through her eyes.

The next day Megha was in her class, Suddenly Vineet came forward and asked the list of total number of participants to take part in **The Inter School Basketball Competition,** all raised their hands nearly it was 15 members, except Megha all raised their hands. The bell rang and all the students went for their lunch break, that time Megha was about to leave and Vineet blocked her way and asked her, 'Why aren't you participating in this game?'. She replied simply to him that, 'You have such brisk and active players in your team and I am not worth for your team '. Then Vineet left her without speaking a word to her. Megha thought THAT'S IT! He is not going to talk with her and he is not going to teach her basketball. And she left him to attend her next class, when it came to last hour, A boy from 5th standard came to inform Megha's teacher that P.E.T Teacher is calling Megha for personal work. Then with her teacher's permission she went to meet the P.E.T sir. He said to Megha that, 'You have been selected for the basketball team and the trainer is Vineet!', she was completely mesmerized on his words, as she was about to reply her opinion to the teacher, Vineet came forward and said "IT'S TIMES FOR THE PRACTISE NOW SIR" Shall I take Megha now. Before leaving them the teacher said,' Ok you can carry on guys!!!! This time our school should score the best my boy!!! Vineet just smiled at him and took MEGHA to the ground for the practice.

Megha had a flying of colors of happiness outside, but inside she was not. The presence of Vineet makes her happy and brave to do anything in her life, and that presence of him made her participate in the match. After that Megha started to love Vineet from the Bottom of her heart truly, but she never expressed her love to him. The match was successful as both the girls and the boys team won the match. Vineet, Megha as well as the entire school members were in great bliss. Then nearly three years passed Megha was 17 now studying 12th standard. Vineet completed his schooling at the same time and joined the college for his higher studies.

Till all this time Megha did not express her immense love to Vineet. Then, years passed and she was not normal like before just doing her degree in English Literature and nor being satisfied with her life, she was running completely like a muddy fog. The only groom that comes to her mind was VINEET! VINEET! VINEET! She refused every groom that had been chosen by her parents. Finally her father asked Megha, 'ARE YOU IN LOVE?' But she doesn't have the exact answer for that, she neither replied YES or NO to her parents. Now Megha is 23 now.

She was at the terrace just watching the chirping birds, listening to her favourite songs through her headset. Suddenly a car stood in front of her house, she stood up and watched WHO IT WAS? Believe it or not shocking to her surprise it was VINEET! with his parents, for a moment she wasn't able to believe in her eyes. Megha was so nervous that she was unable to come down off the terrace. It was so silent from outside after an hour she heard a loud voice MEGHA COME HERE! It was her dad. Megha came silently to the hall were she could see Vineet sitting beside her father talking in a jolly manner, Her father asked her, *SO THIS WAS YOUR ENTIRE SILENCE RIGHT, THESE MANY YEARS THIS WAS THE THING THAT PRICKS YOU A LOT ISN'T IT!* On hearing this word from her father, Megha was not able to control her tears. She went to her room, her mother hugged her tight and said WHY SWEETY! YOU DID NOT INFORMED THIS LOVE STORY AT LEAST TO ME! I WAS YOUR FRIEND MORE THAN A MOTHER TO YOU! Megha said MOM I WAS SO AFRAID OF MY THOUGHT I LOVED HIM SO DEEPLY FROM MY HEART, THE FEAR WAS 'WILL HE EXCEPT MY LOVE', HE NEVER TALKED TO ME LIKE A LOVER, HE JUST BEHAVED LIKE A GOOD FRIEND I DON'T WANT TO RUIN MYSELF FROM HIM COMPLETELY AND I DON'T KNOW WHETHER HIS PARENTS WOULD EXPECT ME OR NOT!! TOTALLY I WAS PUNISHING AND BUILDING A COFFIN TO BURY MY EMOTIONS MOM!!!! Her mother held her tight and was proud of her daughter. Then Vineet came inside the room and asked the permission "MAY I COME IN MY MOTHER-IN-LAW" Megha's Mom just held her tears and said, COME IN MY SON! and she left the room. Megha hugged Vineet so tightly and asked HOW COULD YOU LOVE ME WITHOUT EXPRESSING NOTHING TO ME. Then he said, 'Do you remember one thing? When I hit you on the road side and buy my snacks without bothering you, but when you left I bothered you a lot my dear I liked you at my first site of yours.

First thing was, I need to confirm the same love from you, so I joined your school.

Second thing when I started to watch you through my heart I completely confirmed that you are a silent lover and had a crush on me and I confirmed that it was love.

Third thing before I propose you I should be in a good position so that I could ask your hand to my father-in-law with my parents permission. These many years I have been loving your patience and you too rejected so many people in your life and you were waiting for me without no reason. After conforming all this stuff these many years I waited for this moment in my life "WILL YOU MARRY ME MEGHA?" She simply hugged him and said YES!

The end of the story is for this today's youngest generation world, *the biggest and the most beautiful ecstasy that grows in our life is making life decisions with our parents permission. Because hurting them and making a new life of our own is not permanent ecstasy of growing together, it is like a wholesome of bliss, creation and innovation. So think twice the way of making a beautiful permanent ecstasy in your life. Now feel the same extent of complete sense of beautiful ecstasy through this short story.*

LOVERS BUT DOUBTEDLY FRIENDS

Sounds suspicious right. But in some other cases it works when you need someone who supports you generally but due to hypothetical conditions he prefers to be your best friend not like bestie types but something more than that you can't term them as into an embedded circles they are something made for each other and remains to be a great one till your death bed. Normally this happens, when you unconditionally love a person without expecting anything from them, just a pure soulful love and that is enough for them to make their life an uncountable desire of their own life. Some people say that they really love you or really like you, normally all never show their immense love through their actions, the only thing is they just say and move on. But some do exist like a forever friendly soul who never blames you, never put you down and connects your heart in such a way that you can't afford to lose them at any cause, all they want is just stay connected who ever comes into their life, it is like selfless love, you can able to control a person when you like them or you want them completely according to your self-designed taste. It is done naturally not by tying a rope to just hang over their feelings for your personal needs.

It is simply a sigh of love not relief all the time. You should feel blessed to have such kind of magical partners in your life, if you feel that you don't want to continue them as your friend just grab their inner beauty to lead a beautiful life with them. When you are just travelling with me just make it as an easy point of view not to ruin a great mess with idiotic silly expressions, and formal speechless dialogues. This type of love is something special, not all sorts of people encounter it, it is like a peaceful feeling, selfless and cannot be shared with anyone else. If you least expect it, then my friend you are going through it. Friendship differs totally, the selfless thoughts just make you stand still and get an endless bliss inside you.

Some don't value those feeling due to some stupid people point of view they judge that it is love go and make life with them, but my answer would be no, don't fall so easily just give chance for them too, if you like or the way they like you they won't hurt you generally; instead they guide you and lead you towards a beautiful destiny which you could ever imagine, some say that it is an illogical fantasy, in a relationship nothing is defined equally, just move and go with the a flow but never dare to lose your discipline and self control those who don't value your feelings. If you expect a love or comeback essence of dignity from them then this would create an unwanted mess in your life. Forcing emotional thoughts and magical words never decides your life partner. If you are finding pleasure in it, it's ok, but it should not hurt the other part of the person who is just opposite to you. Never give them hope! Don't make massive drastic punches on their faith, once it is broken then you have to face the ugliest circumstances by yourself. Never plead or blame on a person to continue a broken relationship.

My dear friends if a person leaves you in any part of the relationship which you were continuing just break it, if it seems to be ok, don't move on to the fake part. Show your bad face too, and the other one stays to that extent of your bad part, choose them, don't make a person as you like, choose a partner who never makes you alike.

Now I am going to continue my story-3 which will give you the same pleasure as I have already confessed before.

STORY-3

LOVERS UNDOUBTEDLY FRIENDS-
STEVEN AND JAMIE

Oh my God! Jamie Please stop it's raining! No Steven I can't it's lovely! I feel like a child at this moment. Are you kidding me right now? Just get into the car please Jamie Please!

Okay coming my savage! What did you just call me savage Jamie!

Yes I do! Okay it is getting late shall we move!

Okay Jamie.

Before 5 years………..

Jamie was a peculiar kind of girl. She was a cute and depressed character, like two in one type. Her happiness depends upon her moods which she carries along herself. She spreads bliss and positivity among all her friends and people, but she never supports or tackles her emotional aspects as she does on others. She cares about others ' situations more easily than her own self.

She completed her Master's Degree in English Literature, and was wondering in search of a good job.

....

Hey honey! Have some coffee with my special cookies! It was her roommate Clara.

Please give me some coffee, not cookies now!

Why what happened?

I am not in a mood to prefer your cookies.

You are preferring moods to eat my cookies, literally it is funny Miss. Jamie.

Listen Clara! I am going to fly myself towards New York.

New York! That's great. But Why?

My idea has been approved by them. So the thing is I got a job in New York as a leading communicative client there.

O my god Jamie! That's terrific! All the best my dear.

Hmmm nice!!

Clara! What are you looking into my mail?

Nothing serious, You are appointed to work in IBM. And we found your profile is perfectly matching our site and we are honored to appoint in our company as a self leading project manager.

By: Steven and Team.

Jamie! Do you have the same feeling about this Steven. How could you? It is not working, just cancel this offer we'll find the other job okay!

Clara! What about the name? I know Steven is dead but I will not be disturbed by this name. I am okay. And you see it is the best opportunity to make a great shine in my life, please I want to do that!

Jamie my dear, I know you are bold enough but I know about you clearly you can't forget this man ever in your life, you bother so much for Steven and he is no more, and the place you are going to work with your boss is tagging with this name STEVEN! Is it comfortable for you my dear, if still something pricks you inside just quit or else do whatever you want? You do your best and I know that, keep going honey nothing matters, all the best!

Thank you Clara, you are my best friend and the only true soul on earth I know. See you Catch you later. Getting back to my work.

It was a great day when I met Steven for the first time in my life. He was a charming young guy, bold character and a nice friend of mine from childhood. I always feel safe when he is around me and hanging all the time whenever I feel depressed. One day, we were going to the park, and all of a sudden he knelt before me and said I LOVE YOU JAMIE! I was totally surprised and he was continuing his talk Jamie you and I don't have a family when we were at the early young age, in an old orphanage, we grew up together our thoughts became united and we became friends. I want you totally in my life till my end. Jamie I love you dear!

Oh! Steven I love you too. Both hugged each other and kissed.

When she opened her eyes Steven felt something and became unconscious. Jamie took her car, drove fast towards the hospital. After an hour, the doctor came to Jamie, and said your boyfriend is suffering from Alzheimer Disease, he has to undergo severe medication otherwise things will get worse then we could imagine. He is a peculiar case, most of them are affected by this disease at an earlier age when they are getting old, but this young man is so irrelevant to this case. Jamie! Took him to Doctor Charles, he is a great specialist in treating the Alzheimer diseased people, have hope my dear don't worry. And by the way he is in New York. Be quick in making decisions Jamie.

Okay doctor! I will send him to New York.

In New York, Steven got admitted. Jamie made a hard life in taking care of Steven. But he had no improvement. Slowly he was getting his memories erased and he wasn't able to remember anything, even his own Jamie!

When Jamie came to hospital some man just came to pick up Steven. Shocking in her eyes Jamie leaned forward to watch those seen happening in the hospital, it was Steven's Ex Father.

Hey wait you bloody scoundrel WHERE ARE YOU TAKING MY STEVEN! He is not recovered yet.

Stay away you Bitch! I know.

He beat hard on Jamie's stomach and lifted Steven in their car, meanwhile cops came to the hospital and helped Jamie to rescue.

Leave me! Jamie shouted hard and was chasing Steven's Father's car in a fast mode. The police too were following all the way they could. Within a nanosecond she wasn't able to find Steven's father's car, then without leaving her hope she drove as much fast as she could. Before she could arrive on that spot, she saw more cops and people just gathering like sheep on that spot, as she followed those people on the spot, all the cops arrested Jamie, before she could even react, she asked him what happened? They replied that the car had a great crash. Jamie cried hard to look through the crowd, the car was burning in her eyesight, then Jamie could not feel anything, she fainted.

As she opened her eyes she was in the hospital, Clara doctor and all of them were waiting for Jamie to wake up. Then the doctor asked Jamie to take rest and Clara came close to my side.

Hey Clara what happened to my Steven! Is he okay!

No Jamie, he is not ok, in fact he is no more! And she hugged tight, crying to say this news to Jamie.

Jamie! Doctor! Doctor! Jamie is becoming unconscious, please be quick!

Doctor! Is she alright?

Yes, she is, but don't tell the news that she can't bear herself, make herself feel comfortable and strong so that she is able to forgive her past moment to live a brighter future, all will be fine one day trust me.

After 5 years.......

Clara see you soon! I am going to do my work peacefully, do call me you idiot!

Okay mam, Ha! Ha! Take care of yourself, love you so much Jamie!

I love you too Clara! Miss you bye.

Within a few hours she reached New York. She was feeling something satisfied by herself in doing a great job here. Some of them just received Jamie! Through the airport in the most costliest car Bugatti La Voiture, she opened her mouth wide open to see such a costliest car in front of her, at first she felt really shy to get in and when they compelled her to get inside the car, she felt herself like a crowned queen, then she reached New Cross lane street and the car stopped in a spot. Some of their managers just led herself towards the hotel room, which was a fully lavish furnishing hotel which she had not visited till her lifetime.

She entered the room, and had a great feast for her dinner. She went to the balcony and was seeing the whole New York in a tiny eyesight, all were looking tiny as she was on her 12th floor. She looked up to kiss her

Steven from the sky, it would be a better life when I have you now in my life Honey. Then she could hear a calling bell just ringing outside. It was nearly 9.30 pm.

Jamie peeped in through her camera control guard to see who is standing outside. It was her manager Willie. Jamie opened the door and told him to get in.

Mam! Sorry to disturb you.

It's okay. Get in.

Mam. Tomorrow our team is going to meet you including Steven Sir.

(whenever she hears that name, she feels her goosebumps)

Mam! Is it fine?

Yes. I am. Continue.

I came here to inform you that tomorrow is a sharp 7 o'clock. We will be receiving you from your hotel room, so be ready with all of your things and be prepared mam.

O well thank you, Willie.

Welcome mam.

Next day,

6.00 am.

O! Jamie I am proud of you. Congrats for your first day, when you are going to join.

Today at 7.00 by the morning I will be joining them. Okay! Clara love you. I have to go now bye!

Bye! Dear.

In the office.

Good morning Mam. Mr. Steven will be meeting you with his team in a couple of minutes. Please be seated.

O Thank you.

Some men just surrounded Steven, and within a second he rushed into the room.

Miss Jamie, your turn.

Jamie was so excited to enter the room. She walked straight to the room of Steven. She entered the room and saw a huge hall with lots of men, in that group she was the only woman sitting among them. All of them just introduced themselves, for half an hour it was a boring lecture of all.

After that lecture Jamie got selected in all rounds and the final one was the interview session.

Jamie was really excited from inside but she wasn't able to control herself, after that she got a couple of times to get a tea break.

That break made her call Clara.

Hey Clara!

Oh! Hi, How is your work going on? Is it all okay my dear!

All fine! You know I have cleared each round of myself successfully, and I am happy to say to you that I am the only woman working on this project, but still I need to attend a casual interview, after that my dream will come very soon Clara!

That seems you are on cloud nine, isn't it?

Yep! Hope all goes well.

For sure dear all will be fine, all the best for your interview dear!

Thanks! Ok I have to go bye.

Bye dear!

(Both hung their phone)

After that call she was waiting to meet her group of team members, all entered the big hall, Jamie gracefully entered the hall and took her seat with her group.

Miss Jamie! Your turn is eleven, so you have to wait for another half an hour.

No! problem Mam. Thank you.

You're welcome, Miss Jamie. Please take your seat.

After half an hour. Her turn came to visit Mr. Steven for an interview.

Jamie entered the room, with a great breath and she was talking to herself like a manthra like, YOU CAN DO IT JAMIE GOOD LUCK!

As she looked up to see the Steven, she became in an astonished tone. Her heart skipped for a moment, she felt like she can't breathe on her own, her toes and eyes became freezed in a nanoseconds.

Good evening Miss Jamie please be seated, shall we start. Hello Jamie Are you alright, Is everything okay.

Jamie!!

Oh! I apologize sir.

Okay go ahead.

After 15 minutes…..

Jamie! You are a highly talented girl, and you are appointed to our company. This office is yours from tomorrow, my best wishes to you, good luck!

Thank you sir.

Jamie ! One sec, have we met earlier before. Because I had a suspicious feeling on you when I met you before my interview. Do we know each other earlier?

No! sir. Certainly not.

Then why you were astonished at first, when you saw me at first sight!

Oh! Nothing sir. You looked exactly as my friend, so I was surprised, nothing serious sir.

Okay! But I feel we have already met before, I never felt such strange behavior before I could meet a girl like you, something pricks me so strangely. Okay! Nothing more serious talk, good luck Miss Jamie, have a nice day.

Thank you sir.

As Jamie left the room. She felt a great pain in her heart, surprisingly she wasn't able to believe that he was her own Steven. She cried so hard in the washroom, patted her hands on the wall, tightly closed her mouth so hard that her sound could not reach out. After that she left the wash room and drove fast to her home.

Hey Jamie! You took a whole day to come back home, is it all fine dear!

Oh! Clara! That one word she sounded so terrible and hugged Clara so tightly before Clara could react over Jamie's reaction. Jamie explained everything about Steven, Clara too cried a lot as she explained exactly what happened to her in her office.

Enough Jamie! Quit your job or else explain everything about your love and the tragic incident to Steven, you have to do something to withdraw the situation dear!

I can't!

Why? You don't love Steven anymore, what happened to you, earlier we thought he was dead, now he is alive, how could he! It is like a blank narrow thought! I can't believe he is still alive, if he was then why he could not reach out to you, certainly he is an insane man.

No! Clara, you misunderstood him, he was suffering from Alzheimer already, he doesn't remember anything even me!

So funny Jamie! Then why did he say that he met you before, it was a great chance to explain your situation and it would be an even better day of yours!

Yes! Clara, you are right, but I have to say something more about that, as I was about to explain something to him, he got a call from his wife, he was talking so happily with her and I also watched his daughter photo too on his table, it was completely a sweet family, if I opened my mouth there, I could definitely ruin his beautiful family, I don't want to do this to him.

That's why I remain speechless.

Oh! Jamie I am proud of you, but feeling really sad for both of you.

It is true but I am fine that he is alive, nothing could not spare him and he would live happily ever after, loving someone is not just a great deal but if you still love him even the situation separates you that really makes a great sense. I am sad that my love story is incomplete, but Clara trust me, I am much better to see him with a happy family and I am damn sure about that my love is so pure for him, my prayers will protect him forever, I may not be a wife for him but I will be a trustable best friend throughout my lifetime!

****